AWE-SOME DAYS

Poems about the Jewish Holidays

by MARILYN SINGER

illustrated by
DANA WULFEKOTTE

Dial Books For Young Readers

FOLLOWING THE HOLIDAYS

This is the year

we will follow the holidays,

the ones we know well,

the one we do not.

Days full of questions,

why, how, and what?

Days when we're thoughtful,

days we are loud.

Days we can do better,

days we feel proud.

In the light, in the dark,

in the temple, the park.

In our home, in the sukkah,

fretting over the weather,

this is the year

we will follow the holidays.

This is the year

we will spend them together.

ROSH HASHANAH

Apples dipped in honey.

Walnut cake with syrup.

Dates and pomegranates.

Each a Rosh Hashanah treat,

    so the New Year will be sweet.

And I will try to be sweeter, too.

And not just in temple,

    when I hear the shofar sound.

But outside and after,

    in all of the seasons,

    in my home, in my school, on the busy playground,

    with my classmates, with my friends,

    with my father and my mother,

    with my clever older sister and my funny little brother,

      who are sometimes mean and sometimes not

        and sometimes in the way.

I will try to be sweeter.

I'm beginning today.

Rosh Hashanah, a two-day fall holiday (though some observe it for one day), marks the beginning of the Jewish New Year. On this holiday, it is said that God opens the Book of Life and judges every person's behavior. In the synagogue, the shofar—a ram's horn—is blown in a pattern of long and short blasts, to say "Wake up! You can change yourself and the world for everyone's good!" Jews have ten days—called the High Holy Days or the Days of Awe—between this holiday and Yom Kippur to think about how to be and do better and to apologize to people they have wronged. Some practice tashlich: They symbolically cast off their sins and bad behavior by throwing stones or bits of bread into a river, lake, or other body of water.

At home, families and friends may gather for a feast, including challah bread and sweet foods such as apples and honey to usher in a sweet year. Many people eat pomegranates with the wish "May we be as full of merits as the pomegranate is full of seeds."

YOM KIPPUR

No cake, no honey,

and for me,

no soccer, no TV.

On this day so serious

      (and a little mysterious),

I give them up.

On this day I say I am sorry

for any unkind thing I've done

      (even when nobody's seen it).

I promise not to do it again

      and I pray

that on more than just this awe-some day,

I really mean it.

Yom Kippur, which ends the Days of Awe, is also called the Day of Atonement. It is the holiest of the High Holy Days. Many people who do not celebrate other Jewish holidays will spend this one in temple. At nightfall when the service ends, there is one long blast of the shofar to mark the closing of the Book of Life.

On this day, adults fast. Children under the age of thirteen are not required to give up food, but they (as well as grown-ups) may give up things that they enjoy in order to concentrate on atoning—on recognizing and righting any wrongs they've done. Kids are taught not only to say "I'm sorry," but to mean it and to ask for forgiveness. After sundown, people break their fast and some begin to build a sukkah for the next holiday, Sukkot.

SUKKOT

In our beautiful sukkah, hung with gourds and dried corn from the farm stand,

    I take the bundled branches

        of palm, myrtle, and willow

            in my right hand

                for the first time.

In my left is the citron,

        so lemony-delicious, I sniff and sniff.

"Don't drop it," Mama warns.

"I won't," I say, holding tight to the etrog

        while I wave the lulav

        forward, right, back,

        left, up, down,

reciting blessings,

thinking how lucky we are to live here together

        on this generous planet.

"Good job." Mama beams.

Tonight, after we feast and laugh

        and watch the stars shine through the roof

of our beautiful sukkah, I will fall asleep and dream

that I am holding the etrog, waving the lulav

        in that place I will someday visit,

           that land where my cousins live,

      where those palms, myrtles, willows,

           and lemony-delicious citrons came from

      and where they still grow.

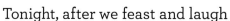

When the Israelites traveled to the Promised Land, they gathered and slept in huts or tents. During Sukkot, Jews remember that journey by building a temporary shelter called a sukkah under an open sky. A sukkah has at least three walls and the roof must be made of natural materials. It is often decorated with leaves, vegetables, fruits, and flowers. People will eat in the sukkah for seven days and may even sleep there. They welcome family and friends, as well as the spirits of figures from the Bible. And they think about people, past and present, who had to wander and take shelter wherever they could, as well as the good fortune of having a permanent home.

Sukkot is also linked to harvest time in Israel and it celebrates the earth's gifts and resources. As a reminder of their connection to the environment, people recite prayers while they shake a lulav—a bundle of palm, myrtle, and willow branches—and hold an etrog—a citron, which is a type of citrus fruit. The lulav and etrog are often shipped to America from Israel, where these plants are grown.

SHEMINI ATZERET

Grandpa calls it an "almost holiday,"

this day after Sukkot

(although Grandma disagrees and says

it's a full holiday for sure).

No more waving the lulav, holding the etrog.

Different blessings, different prayers.

My favorite is the one for rain,

which we sometimes need more of

and sometimes need less,

but I kind of hope we don't get tonight,

hiding the stars,

pattering through the roof,

down the dangling gourds and corn cobs

onto my bed,

onto my head,

on this, my last night in the beautiful sukkah.

Perhaps less familiar than other holidays, Shemini Atzeret is the day after Sukkot. The name means both a day of solemn gathering and of cessation because it ends Sukkot. In Israel, this day is combined with Simchat Torah as one holiday. However, elsewhere it is celebrated as a full holiday in its own right. People still eat and sleep in the sukkah, but they do not shake the lulav or recite some of the blessings. They do say a special prayer for rain to help crops grow and provide water for people and animals, especially in parts of the world where there is often drought.

SIMCHAT TORAH

Wave the flags!

Sing the songs!

Watch merriment abound!

They're marching with the Torah,
  seven times around.

Listen to the women read,
  listen to the men.

Listen as the Torah ends
  and then begins again.

Blessings on my family,
  friends and neighbors, too.

We are strong together
  and the Torah is our glue!

Simchat Torah ("rejoicing in the Torah") is the day after Shemini Atzerat. During this joyful holiday, Jews finish reading the Torah—the first five books of the Bible, which contain the main Jewish laws and traditions—and then start reading it again, beginning with the story of creation. In the synagogue, people sing, dance, and parade with the Torah scrolls seven times around the room. This parade is called the hakafot and some congregations perform it on Shemini Atzerat as well. Children join the march, sometimes carrying flags, and they receive a special blessing. In Israel and other places, the celebration may go on out-doors late into the evening.

HANUKKAH

Candles and miracles,

chocolate gelt

    (wrapped in foil so it doesn't melt).

Dreidels and latkes,

maybe sufganiyot

    (don't get jam on my brand-new coat!).

I love our old menorah.

I love each song we sing.

I love the lights

on all eight nights.

    (I wish they would burn till it's spring!)

Many people, Jews and non-Jews alike, are familiar with Hanukkah. They know that it falls near the winter solstice and that a candle is lit in a Hanukkah menorah—a special candelabra—for each of eight nights (the ninth candle is used to light the others). They may also be aware that people eat delicious potato pancakes called latkes. In Israel and other places, the special food is sufganiyot—jelly-filled donuts. But many people don't know the story behind the holiday. It is about a bad king who forbade Jews to study the Torah and to worship in the Second Temple in ancient Jerusalem. A group of Jews called the Maccabees rebelled, conquered the king's army, and took back the temple. They cleansed and returned it to the Jewish people. The story continues with a miracle. The Maccabees found only enough oil to light the lamp there for one day. But amazingly, the oil lasted for eight days and nights. That is why on this holiday Jews light one candle for each of the eight evenings and eat foods fried in oil.

On Hanukkah, children also get gifts and play with tops called dreidels. The Hebrew letters on the dreidel stand for the phrase "A great miracle happened there" (in Israel, "here" is used instead of "there"). During the game, kids bet "gelt"— money or foil-wrapped chocolate coins—and win or lose, depending on what they spin. There are a number of explanations about the dreidel game. One is that children were studying the Torah in secret. If a king's man got too close, they would take out tops and pretend they were just playing.

Tu B'Shevat

There, where my cousins live,

the almond trees they planted are already blooming,

their pink and white blossoms beckoning bees.

Here, the ground is still frozen,

and the only pink and white flowers

are the plastic ones in our neighbors' cheerful window box.

But today, in the heart of winter, we will celebrate this Festival of the Trees,

eating almonds, dried figs, apricots, prunes,

and even etrog jam from last Sukkot.

We will bury birch seeds in pots

and wait to see them sprout near the windowsill.

Then, one sunny day when they are big enough,

we will give some to our neighbors,

    plant some in our yard,

if not by Passover,

then surely in time

    for Shavuot.

In much of the U.S., January and February are deep winter. But in Israel, spring is beginning. Tu B'Shevat, or Jewish Arbor Day, is known as the "New Year of Trees." On this day, people plant trees—or seeds indoors if they live where the ground is frozen—and learn how important these are to the environment. They find other ways to appreciate nature and the environment as well, such as having a special meal of fruits and nuts that trees and other plants provide.

PURIM

My brother asks why I love Purim,

just why I love this holiday.

I give him a tickle behind his ears,

and here is what I say:

You can be the hero, the king or the queen.

Today you don't have to be you.

It's time for this story, so grab a noisemaker.

And when they say Haman's name, boo!

You can give presents to family and friends

and donate to a great charity.

You can nosh on hamantaschen

(as long as you save some for me!).

You can visit a carnival, or go to a play.

Maybe you will be the star.

You can be serious, you can be silly.

Today you can be who you are.

Queen Esther is one of the Bible's great heroes. The Book of Esther was originally written on a megillah (a scroll), and then included in the Hebrew Bible. Purim applauds her bravery. She was married to King Ashasuerus, who didn't know that she was Jewish. Esther's cousin, Mordecai, refused to bow down to the king's advisor, Haman. Furious, Haman wanted to get rid of Mordecai and all of the other Jews in Persia. When Esther learned of his plot, she spoke to the king about Haman's evil plan, admitting that she too was Jewish, and she asked him to spare her fellow Jews. The king declared that Haman be punished instead.

Today, Purim is a joyous holiday on which people hold carnivals and dress up as figures from the Book of Esther or in other costumes. In the synagogue, they boo and use noisemakers called groggers when they hear Haman's name. They also give gifts to the poor, exchange food baskets and gifts with friends and neighbors, and eat pastries called hamantaschen, which are shaped like Haman's three-cornered hat.

PASSOVER

I practice, practice every day so I can get it right

when it's time for me to ask just why we say this night

is different from all others: Why this matzoh? And these herbs—

why dip them twice? And why recline (that's one of my new verbs!)?

Now we're at the seder and it's my turn to shine.

I start the questions perfectly. It's going really fine.

And then I get to Number Three. What happens isn't nice.

I don't ask why we dip herbs twice; I ask why we "drip ice."

My sister grins, my father laughs like I've said something cute.

My brother whoops, my grandpa coughs, both my cousins hoot.

Then Mom says with a poker face, "When Israel fled the threat

of Pharaoh's wrath, I'm sure they dreamed of something cool and wet.

"Of calm oases in the desert, or with imagination,

snowy mountains, icy lakes to take a long vacation."

And then I have to giggle, too, and go to Question Four.

Everyone says that I did great and Dad yells out, "Encore!"

But I decline (as we recline) though I feel like a winner.

I want to hear about the Plagues. I want to have our dinner,

then find the Afikomen—I might get to it first.

But even if my brother does, I'm so happy, I could burst!

Long ago in Egypt, a cruel pharaoh enslaved the Jewish people. Their leader, Moses, asked the pharaoh to release them. When the ruler refused, Moses said that God would call down terrible plagues, which would afflict the Egyptians but "pass over" the homes of the Jews. After the tenth plague, Pharaoh at last told the Jews they could leave the country. They left so quickly they had no time to leaven their dough—to let it rise into bread. Instead, they made flat crackers called matzoh and fled. But soon Pharaoh sent his army to bring them back. When the Jews reached the Red Sea, they prayed for a miracle. The sea parted and they were able to race through. As they reached the other side, the waters closed. Pharaoh had lost—and the Jews were free.

That is the story Jews read each year from a text called the Haggadah during the special dinner called a seder, which is held the first (and, in some households, second) night of Passover. There are many editions of the Haggadah, and Jews read and discuss it to express their own wishes for freedom. Traditionally, the seder includes a number of rituals, such as explanations about symbolic foods on the seder plate and children asking the Four Questions. These questions begin with "Why is this night different from all other nights?" Then the speaker asks why on this night: we eat matzoh instead of leavened bread; we eat bitter herbs; we dip the herbs twice, in salt water and in a sweet fruit mixture; and we eat reclining instead of sitting upright. During the seder, someone hides a matzoh called the Afikomen, which the children have to find in order to receive a reward. Some people think this game came about to keep the kids awake until the end of the long seder.

ISRAEL INDEPENDENCE DAY

Last Fourth of July, our cousins sent a picture,

smiling faces peering over the top

of an American flag,

and at the ends,

the littlest ones holding sparklers.

This fifth day of Iyar

(which is sometimes April, this year May)

my brother and sister and I send a picture,

smiling faces peering over the top

of an Israeli flag,

and at each end,

Mom and Dad eating falafel.

Dad's chin is white with tahini.

Our cousins text back one word:

Mapeet.

It isn't till later I learn what it means:

Napkin.

On May 15, 1948, Israel declared its independence as a country. On the Jewish calendar, that date fell on the fifth day of the month of Iyar. Now, depending on the year, this national holiday—Yom Ha'atzmaut—is celebrated in April or May on the Western calendar. In Israel, there are official and non-official ceremonies, including parades, fireworks, dancing, and torch lightings. People display Israeli flags and have picnics and especially barbecues. Outside of Israel, Jews may celebrate their spiritual or cultural connection to Israel on Yom Ha'atzmaut with flags, festivities, and Middle Eastern food such as falafel—fried chickpea balls covered with sesame sauce known as tahini. Many will acknowledge both the joy and the political complications that persist to this day.

LAG B'OMER

Ever since he learned

that our cousins shoot arrows

on this holiday,

my brother is so excited.

Ever since my sister discovered

she can get a short haircut

on this holiday,

my sister is delighted.

Ever since I heard

about the bonfires in Israel

on this holiday,

I want to build one, too.

But we just have a barbecue.

Yet with singing and s'mores,

dancing merrily outdoors,

I discover that it will do.

For many people over many centuries, numbers have had special—often mystical—meanings. The number seven, in particular, is mentioned many times in the Bible: seven days of creation, seven days in a week, seven days to celebrate some of the holidays, etc. In the Torah, Jews are instructed to count forty-nine days—seven weeks—between Passover (the festival of freedom) and Shavuot (the receiving of the Torah). This time is known as the Omer. It is a solemn time during which some Jews do not have weddings or other celebrations, buy new clothes, or get haircuts. Why is it a period of sadness? Some say there was once a great plague during Omer that affected many people. Others say that ancient Israelites may have been worried about their crops. In any case, there is one day during Omer when people get to celebrate—Lag B'Omer.

On this, the thirty-third day, some believe that the plague stopped and so people rejoiced. Other stories about the festivities involve two famous teachers. Thousands of years ago, the Romans forbade the teaching of the Torah. But Rabbi Akiva continued to teach the Torah in secret. His students pretended to be hunters and carried bows and arrows into the woods, where they met with the rabbi to study. One of Rabbi Akiva's students was Rabbi Shimon Bar Yochai, who is thought to have written the Zohar, part of the body of Jewish mysticism known as Kabbalah. When he died, it's said that his house was filled with a holy wall of fire and light.

To honor these stories, on Lag B'Omer children get to play with toy bows and rubber-tipped arrows. People light bonfires, go hiking, and dance. Some children and adults may visit the barber or salon for a new do. And some may choose this day to get married.

SHAVUOT

My little brother is standing on a ladder.

"We got it, we got it," he shouts,

     wearing Mom's bathrobe and Dad's Purim beard,

     holding up the scrolls Grandpa gave him last October.

"You are not Moses and that ladder is not Mount Sinai," I say,

     then realize I've promised to be sweet

         (well, at least sweeter).

"But this is the Torah," he declares,

     "and today we are all Moses!"

When he hands me the beard,

     it takes a moment

         before I nod at my little brother's wisdom

and put it on.

Shavuot, which occurs seven weeks after the beginning of Passover, has been called "the most important Jewish holiday you never heard of." It is said that on that day thousands of years ago, Moses received the Torah on Mount Sinai. To observe this event, people stay up all night on the eve of the holiday to study the Torah.

Like several Jewish holidays, Shavuot was originally a harvest festival celebrating the wheat harvest and the gathering of first fruits. Today, in some Israeli congregations, the first fruits are brought to the temple with much singing and dancing. There and elsewhere, synagogues and homes are decorated with branches, green plants, and flowers. People also eat dairy products, such as blintzes (thin pancakes rolled up with cheese and sometimes fruit) and cheesecake. Why? One explanation involves the Jewish dietary laws found in the Torah. These laws explain which meat can be eaten, how animals must be handled, and that meat and dairy products cannot be consumed at the same time.

When Moses read the laws to his people, they hadn't had time to deal properly with meat, so they ate dairy instead. In many congregations, Confirmation, a graduation ceremony from formal Jewish education for teens, is held on this holiday.

TISHA B'AV and YOM HA SHOAH

Can a holiday be sad?

Temples destroyed, lives lost.

We remember the cost.

Can a holiday be sad?

People displaced, wars begun

by decree, by the gun.

Can a holiday be sad?

So much broken, such joy ended.

And yet, we hope things can be mended.

Reflecting, rebuilding,

we work to make things right,

to move away from darkness,

to move into the light.

Yom Ha Shoah (Holocaust Remembrance Day), held in April or May, is also a day of mourning and remembrance. In the 1930s, Adolf Hitler convinced the German people that Jews, as well as other groups including Catholics, Romany, LGBTQ, and the disabled, must be eliminated. This horrifying period is known as the Holocaust. It terminated with the end of World War II in 1945. Yom Ha Shoah is a day to learn history—and never to forget its bitter lessons.

Tisha B'Av, which takes place in August, has been called the saddest day on the Jewish calendar. It is said that both Holy Temples in Jerusalem were destroyed on this day, the First by the Babylonians and the Second by the Romans. Other terrible events took place on Tisha B'Av as well: In Biblical times, Jews began their forty years of wandering in the desert; years later, they were expelled from England and then from Spain. On this day of mourning, people remember these events. They think and talk about how to end hatred.

Tu B'Av

Since she learned

there's another kind of Valentine's Day

our cousins celebrate,

my sister has been trying to say

"I love you" in Hebrew.

Sometimes she gets it right.

Sometimes she doesn't.

But we all know what she means

and we all say it back.

Sometimes we get it wrong.

But the truth is, even then,

with hugs and kisses,

we *always* get it right.

In ancient times, on a day in July or August at the start of the grape harvest, young women put on white clothing and danced in the vineyards in hopes of meeting a mate. For centuries, this festival was mostly forgotten. But more recently, especially in Israel, Tu B'Av has become popular as "Jewish Valentine's Day." It's a romantic day for marriage proposals and weddings when people sing, dance, and say "I love you" with flowers, cards, chocolates, and, of course, words.

SHABBAT

"What is that?" asks my little brother
 one Saturday night at Aunt Hannah's house,
where we've never been before.
"Havdalah, to end Shabbat," she replies,
 pointing to the braided candle,
 the fancy cup,
 the silver box that smells like the cookies
 Dad sometimes bakes.
I know about beginning the Sabbath.
We light the candles, wave our hands in the glow,
 sing the blessing, share the meal.

Once I even made a rhyme:
I holla for challah,
let loose for grape juice!
which my brother thought was funny.
But I didn't know we could do something special
to send us off
to dream of spices and shadows
in the new week.

Shabbat (Sabbath) is a day of rest—and the only special time mentioned in the Ten Commandments: "Remember the Sabbath day and keep it holy." In Judaism, it begins on Friday night and ends on Saturday evening. Just before sundown, people light candles. Many wave their hands over them to welcome the Sabbath and bring light into themselves. Then they cover their eyes and say blessings over the candles. They bless wine (or grape juice) and challah (braided bread) as well and share a festive dinner. They may also find ways to right injustices, one of which is setting aside money to donate to a charity. They may go to synagogue. Some Jews follow strict rules about what they cannot do on the Sabbath, such as traveling by car, cleaning the house, or using computers, phones, and other devices. Others do not observe all of these rules—they may drive to synagogue, watch TV, or garden. Since the idea is to relax and spend time with family, many feel that Shabbat is the time to do whatever helps you unwind and enjoy life.

The Havdalah ("separation") ceremony marks the end of Shabbat. Besides giving blessings over wine, people pass around a good-smelling spice box. They also light a candle that has several wicks, some say to distinguish holy, spiritual things from physical, everyday ones or to show how individuals come together as one on the Sabbath. Lighting this candle leads from the time of rest to the time of work in the new week. Other holidays, such as Rosh Hashanah, Yom Kippur, Sukkot, Passover, and Shavuot, also begin with lighting candles and end with Havdalah.

AMEN!

This was the year
we followed the holidays,
some familiar, some a surprise.
There's still so much to know,
still a ways to go
to be sweeter, to be kinder,
to be grateful, to be wise.
This was the year
we followed the holidays,
learned about each one.
Shall we do it again?
We all say, "Amen!"
We are starting right now—
another year has begun!

A NOTE ABOUT THE JEWISH CALENDAR

Different groups of Jews (or even Jews within groups) in the United States celebrate the holidays in a variety of ways. In addition, Jews from different countries and cultures have their own holiday traditions. However, all Jewish holidays begin and end at sundown. Yet they don't always fall on the same days on the Western (also called Gregorian) calendar, which is based on the solar year. That's because each month of the Jewish calendar is determined by the moon's cycle, which is approximately 29½ days. A Jewish calendar year is eleven days shorter than a Western calendar year. In the past, this created some confusion, so eventually, it was decided that a Jewish month would be either 29 or 30 days and that a thirteenth month would be added periodically. This allowed each holiday to be celebrated within the same few months rather than drifting around the year, so that now, for example, Hanukkah always occurs in the late fall or early winter and Passover in the spring.

WEB RESOURCES

www.bimbam.com/judaism-101/jewish-holidays/

www.chabad.org/holidays/default_cdo/jewish/holidays.htm

www.jewfaq.org/holiday0.htm

www.myjewishlearning.com/?s=holidays

pjlibrary.org/holidays

reformjudaism.org/jewish-holidays

For Yoni Bock and Ron Kaplan

With thanks to consultants Bob Aronson (Senior Development Advisor at the Jewish Federation of Metropolitan Detroit), Steve Aronson, Michelle Bayuk, Yoni Bock, Rabbi Dena Feingold (Beth Hillel Temple, Kenosha, WI), Ron Kaplan, Rabbi Marc Katz (Temple Ner Tamid, Bloomfield, NJ), Lisa Schyck-Aronson, Lawson Shadburn, Lisa Silverman (Former Director, Burton Sperber Jewish Community Library of Los Angeles), Leah Susskind (Co-director at the Chabad Jewish Center of Novi, MI), Susan Tuchman, and Tal Tuchman, and also to my editor, Lauri Hornik, and the good folks at Penguin Young Readers

—M.S.

For Grandma and Grandpa

—D.W.

DIAL BOOKS FOR YOUNG READERS

An imprint of Penguin Random House LLC, New York

First published in the United States of America by Dial Books for Young Readers, an imprint of Penguin Random House LLC, 2022

Text copyright © 2022 by Marilyn Singer ✿ Illustrations copyright © 2022 by Dana Wulfekotte

Visit us online at penguinrandomhouse.com.

Library of Congress Cataloging-in-Publication Data is available.

Manufactured in Spain

EST

ISBN 9780593324691

1 3 5 7 9 10 8 6 4 2

Design by Jason Henry ✿ Text set in Archer
The art for this book was created using pencil and then colored digitally.